This
PJ BOOK
belongs to

_____

_____

PJ Library®

JEWISH BEDTIME STORIES and SONGS

To my mother and father and their
weekly visitors, Sadie and Mary.
And as always and forever, to Gill,
Sarah and Ben. – GC

Text copyright © 2013 by Cary Fagan
Illustrations copyright © 2013 by Gary Clement
Published in Canada and the USA in 2013 by Groundwood Books
This edition of *Oy, Feh, So?* was printed for PJ Library in 2018
ISBN 978-1-55498-378-0

Groundwood Books / House of Anansi Press
groundwoodbooks.com

We acknowledge for their financial support of our publishing program the Canada
Council for the Arts, the Ontario Arts Council, and the Government of Canada.

 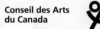

Canada Council **Conseil des Arts**
for the Arts **du Canada**

ONTARIO ARTS COUNCIL
CONSEIL DES ARTS DE L'ONTARIO
an Ontario government agency
un organisme du gouvernement de l'Ontario

With the participation of the Government of Canada
Avec la participation du gouvernement du Canada | Canadä

The illustrations were done in pen and ink and watercolor
on Arches 300 lb. hot press paper.
Design by Michael Solomon
Printed and bound in Canada
101830.6K2/B1336/A7

MIX
Paper from
responsible sources
FSC® C016245
FSC
www.fsc.org

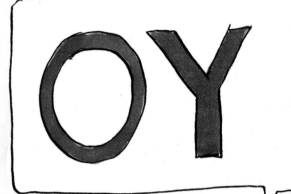

CARY FAGAN   PICTURES BY GARY CLEMENT

GROUNDWOOD BOOKS

HOUSE OF ANANSI PRESS

TORONTO   BERKELEY

Every Sunday my two aunts and my uncle came to visit. Their names were Aunt Essy, Aunt Chanah and Uncle Sam. They drove up after lunch in Uncle Sam's old Lincoln and parked in the driveway.

From the front window, I watched with my brother and sister. Aunt Essy, Aunt Chanah and Uncle Sam got out of the car and walked slowly up the path.

"Do you think they'll say something different today?" my sister asked.

"Not a chance," my brother answered.

They came in without knocking and headed straight for the living room. Aunt Essy sat down in the big armchair with a sigh. Aunt Chanah groaned as she lowered herself onto one end of the sofa.

Uncle Sam winced as he
dropped onto the other end.
"Oy," said Aunt Essy.
"Feh," said Aunt Chanah.
"So?" said Uncle Sam.
That was *all* they ever said!

Our mother came in to greet them.
"Such beautiful weather," Mom said.
"Oy," said Aunt Essy. "As if I haven't seen nicer."
"Feh," said Aunt Chanah. "It'll probably rain."
"So?" said Uncle Sam. "Is the weather going to make me young again?"

Our father came in, too.

"Do you like the new sofa?" Dad asked.

"Oy," said Aunt Essy. "It looks just like the old one."

"Feh," said Aunt Chanah. "A waste of money."

"So?" said Uncle Sam. "You think I don't feel the springs?"

The same thing! Just like every Sunday!
But today my brother, my sister and I had a plan.
My parents went into the kitchen to make tea.
I ran into the living room.
"Help! Help! Robbers!"

OY

Right behind me came two masked robbers holding wooden swords. Aunt Essy, Aunt Chanah and Uncle Sam watched from their seats. The robbers made me take all the money out of my pockets — a dime, two quarters and three nickels. They put the money into their big sack, laughing gleefully.

"Oy," said Aunt Essy. "Crime these days."

"Feh," said Aunt Chanah. "People are animals."

"So?" said Uncle Sam. "Did you expect different?"

FEH

SO?

Again I ran into the living room.

"Help! Help! A dragon is trying to eat me!"

Right behind me came the terrifying dragon with its big snapping jaws. It began to swallow my leg. It began to swallow my other leg! I waved my arms about.

"Oy," said Aunt Essy. "Such a commotion."

"Feh," said Aunt Chanah. "I never liked pets."

"So?" said Uncle Sam. "Is it worse than my bad stomach?"

Aunt Essy, Aunt
Chanah and Uncle Sam
began to snore.

Once more I ran into the living room.

"Help! Help! Space invaders are trying to take me to their planet!"

The space invaders caught me in their force field. They made me lie down on their transporter carpet. They dragged the carpet toward their spaceship.

"Oy," said Aunt Essy, yawning. "As if we don't have enough trouble on earth."

"Feh," said Aunt Chanah. "They probably have germs."

"So?" said Uncle Sam. "Are they any worse than the robbers?"

Every Sunday the same thing! Every Sunday the same three words!

I was angry. More than angry. I stamped my foot.

"I can't take it anymore," I said.

I grabbed a handful of wool from my mother's knitting basket. I put it on my head.

"Oy!" I said. "Oy, oy, oy!"

My sister looked about and found a pair of toy glasses. She crossed her arms.

"Feh!" she said. "Feh, feh, feh!"

Now it was my brother's turn. He picked up a big pillow and stuffed it under his shirt.

"So?" he said, tipping from one foot to the other. "So, so, so?"

And then our parents came in.

"Stop that right now," Mom said.

"Yes," Dad said. "Stop making fun of your aunts and your uncle."

But Aunt Essy pointed to my brother and started to laugh.

"Oy, look at that! He looks just like you, Sam. He *sounds* just like you!"

"So?" Sam said, also laughing. "What about Chanah? That's just the way she sounds!"

"Feh," said Aunt Chanah, giggling. "And isn't that just like Essy? Her hair? Her voice?"

Aunt Essy, Aunt Chanah and Uncle Sam laughed harder. They laughed until they couldn't breathe. They laughed until tears came to their eyes.

My sister and my brother and I
laughed, too. Even my parents laughed.
They served us tea and macaroons.
Then my aunts and my uncle told us
stories from when they were kids.

It got late.
My aunts and my uncle
got up and went to the door. They got into
the car and rolled down the windows.
"Are you sure you have to go?" I asked.
"Stay a little longer," said my brother.

"Please," said my sister.

"Oy," said Aunt Essy. "Next thing, they'll ask us to move in."

"Feh," said Aunt Chanah. "As if we don't have something better to do."

"So?" said Uncle Sam. "Next Sunday isn't soon enough?"

Uncle Sam backed slowly out of the drive. We waved as the car went up the street, the horn sounding three times. *Honk, honk, honk.*